My Mom's Piano

Nora Ellison

illustrated by
Joel Gennari

PowerKiDS
press

New York

Published in 2019 by The Rosen Publishing Group, Inc.
29 East 21st Street, New York, NY 10010

First Edition

Managing Editor: Nathalie Beullens-Maoui
Editor: Elizabeth Krajnik
Art Director: Michael Flynn
Book Design: Raúl Rodriguez
Illustrator: Joel Gennari

Cataloging-in-Publication Data

Names: Ellison, Nora.
Title: My mom's piano / Nora Ellison.
Description: New York : PowerKids Press, 2019. | Series: Making music! | Includes index.
Identifiers: LCCN ISBN 9781508168164 (pbk.) | ISBN 9781508168140 (library bound) |
ISBN 9781508168171 (6 pack)
Subjects: LCSH: Piano–Juvenile fiction. | Mothers–Juvenile fiction. | Music–Juvenile fiction.
Classification: LCC PZ7.E445 My 2019 | DDC [E]–dc23

Manufactured in the United States of America

CPSIA Compliance Information: Batch #CS18PK. For further information contact Rosen Publishing, New York, New York at 1-800-237-9932

Contents

My family has a piano.

It has black and white keys.

My mom knows
how to play.

She can read music notes.

My mom can play fast!

Her hands slide down the keys.

Her fingers hit the keys.

Kyle is our neighbor.

My mom gives him piano lessons.

Kyle is learning to play Mozart.

He's playing in a recital soon.

On Sunday, we go to church.

My mom plays piano while we sing.

I practice playing the piano after church. I sit on the bench with my mom.

My grandma taught
my mom how
to play piano.

20

Now my mom is teaching me.

I tap the keys and sing.
I love playing piano
with my mom.

Words to Know

bench

keys

music notes

Index